NORTHBROOK PUBLIC LIBRARY
1201 CEDAR LANE
NORTHBROOK, IL 60062

NORTHBROOK PUBLIC LIBRARY

DISCARDED

3 1123 00508 2063

W9-ATT-383

A COSTUME FOR NOAH
A Purim Story

Susan Remick Topek
illustrated by Sally Springer

KAR-BEN COPIES, INC.   ROCKVILLE, MD

For Ron and Judy, Carole and Marty, Kathy and Larry
My wonderful brothers and sisters!
With love,
Your baby sister, Sue

Library of Congress Cataloging-in-Publication Data

Topek, Susan Remick.
A costume for Noah   : a Purim story / Sue Remick Topek :
illustrated by Sally Springer.
     p.   cm.
          Summary: Noah's classmates are busy making costumes for the Purim parade, but he is
preoccupied with the imminent arrival of a new baby.
     ISBN 0-929371-91-7. — ISBN 0-929371-90-9 (pbk).)
     [1. Purim—Fiction. 2. Costume—Fiction. 3. Babies—Fiction. 4. Brothers and
sisters—Fiction.] I. Springer, Sally, ill. II. Title.
PZ7.T64417Co 1995
[E] — dc20
                                                                                    95-26152
                                                                                    CIP
                                                                                    AC

"What should I be for Purim?" Noah asked his teacher on
Monday morning. "I want to be something different this year."

"Do your mommy and daddy have any ideas?" she asked.

"All they can think about is having the new baby." Noah replied.

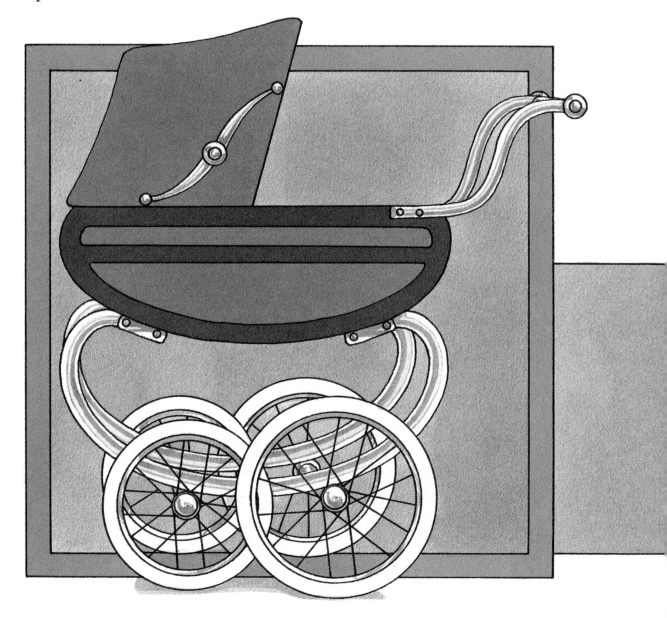

"What's the big megillah about a new baby?" asked David.

"I have three brothers and a sister. We're all dressing up like hamantaschen — strawberry, poppyseed, apricot, prune, and peanut butter."

"Gee, that is different!" exclaimed Noah.

"Speaking of a big megillah, why don't you two help finish the megillah for the bulletin board," the teacher suggested.

Noah colored a picture of Mordechai, but still couldn't think of what to be for Purim.

On Tuesday, everyone made groggers. The classroom was very noisy.

Noah sat next to Dylan. They filled plastic bottles with popcorn kernels and decorated them with colored tissue.

"My dad is making me a king's costume," whispered Dylan.

"I don't know what to be," sighed Noah. "Nobody at my house is thinking about Purim. Everybody is waiting for the new baby."

"You could be a king like me," suggested Dylan.

"I was King Ahashuerus last year," replied Noah. "I want to be something different this year."

On Wednesday, Noah's class made hamantaschen. Everyone was busy measuring, stirring, and rolling out the dough.

"Did your mom have the baby yet?" asked Saul, as he and Noah counted out chocolate chips.

"No, no baby yet," said Noah sadly, "and no costume either."

"I'm going to be a soccer player," said Saul. "Why don't you be a baseball player, and you can wear your old uniform."

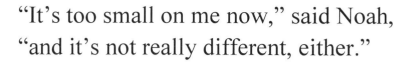

"It's too small on me now," said Noah,
"and it's not really different, either."

On Thursday, Noah helped decorate the shalach manot baskets the class would take to the nursing home.

"Did your new baby come yet?" Leah asked Noah as she spread glitter on her basket.

"Not yet," Noah sighed. "Leah, what are you going to be for Purim?"

"A butterfly with giant, colorful wings!" Leah smiled.

"Wow!" exclaimed Noah. "I want to be something different like that."

On Friday, everyone came to school in costume. There were kings and queens, butterflies and bunnies.

Everyone lined up for the parade. Everyone but Noah.
Noah wasn't in school.

Suddenly, Noah ran into the room.

"We're so glad you're here," said the teacher. "But where is your costume?"

Noah smiled a big smile. "I have something really wonderful, really great, and really different to be for Purim this year."

He took off his jacket and showed the class his new sweatshirt.

"I have a new baby sister," Noah said proudly. "So this year
I'm a BIG BROTHER for Purim."